Tooth, Claw & Heart

Exalting the Lupine Rampant

Edward Martin III

Published by **Hellbender Media**
rare and voracious entertainment
HellbenderMedia.com

There is nothing new in the world, only ancient things and their soft whispers.

This book is dedicated to those among us who struggle with who we really are and who we can become.

The answer is yes.

The time is now.

I believe in you.

Special thanks to

Sandra Elliott
Curtis Threadgold
Taunya Gren
Dylan Martin
Jeffrey Stackhouse
Tara Walker
Michelle Krause
Amber Bariaktari
Katrina Martin

Dankon, por via forto!

Prologue

In the night I hear their voices raised in chorus toward a silent swollen moon. No one is born knowing what to do, knowing how to act, knowing which pit to step over. They have questions. So many questions. Also, there are the other voices, and those voices offer answers, insight, wisdom, and blood.

So herein are the things I have heard, the advice, the thoughts, the considerations, and the blossoming strength. I listened (and still do) to those voices, and as fast as I can, I bring their words here.

There is magic in this book. It doesn't matter where you start, or where you end. Bend your mind and might toward what you most want to understand, and open the book at random.

There is your answer.

May it bring you peace, joy, and prey.

*You will eventually die, but don't be
vampire-glum about it.*

*During your time of living, you
are an extraordinary
force of nature.*

If it smells bad, it is bad.

*Most of the people who think
"killing humans is a bad thing"
are human.*

It's a matter of self-interest.

*But you don't have to
subscribe to that.*

Keep your fur clean.

If you are going to spend your life with another person, make sure it's someone who understands that you can — and will — change quickly.

Keep your teeth clean.

Evidentiary science is a thing.

*Change the world — eat those
who make problems.*

Lycanthropy may not be
elegant, but it's honest.

Own that.

Keep a tidy house.

Remember that Transformation
enhances all your senses.

The main difference between a claw and a hand is this: hands can lie.

A claw is always honest.

*If you are grumpy and irritable
before your Transformation,
make some alone time.*

*Focus, meditate, and
be in yourself.*

Belly rubs are the best!

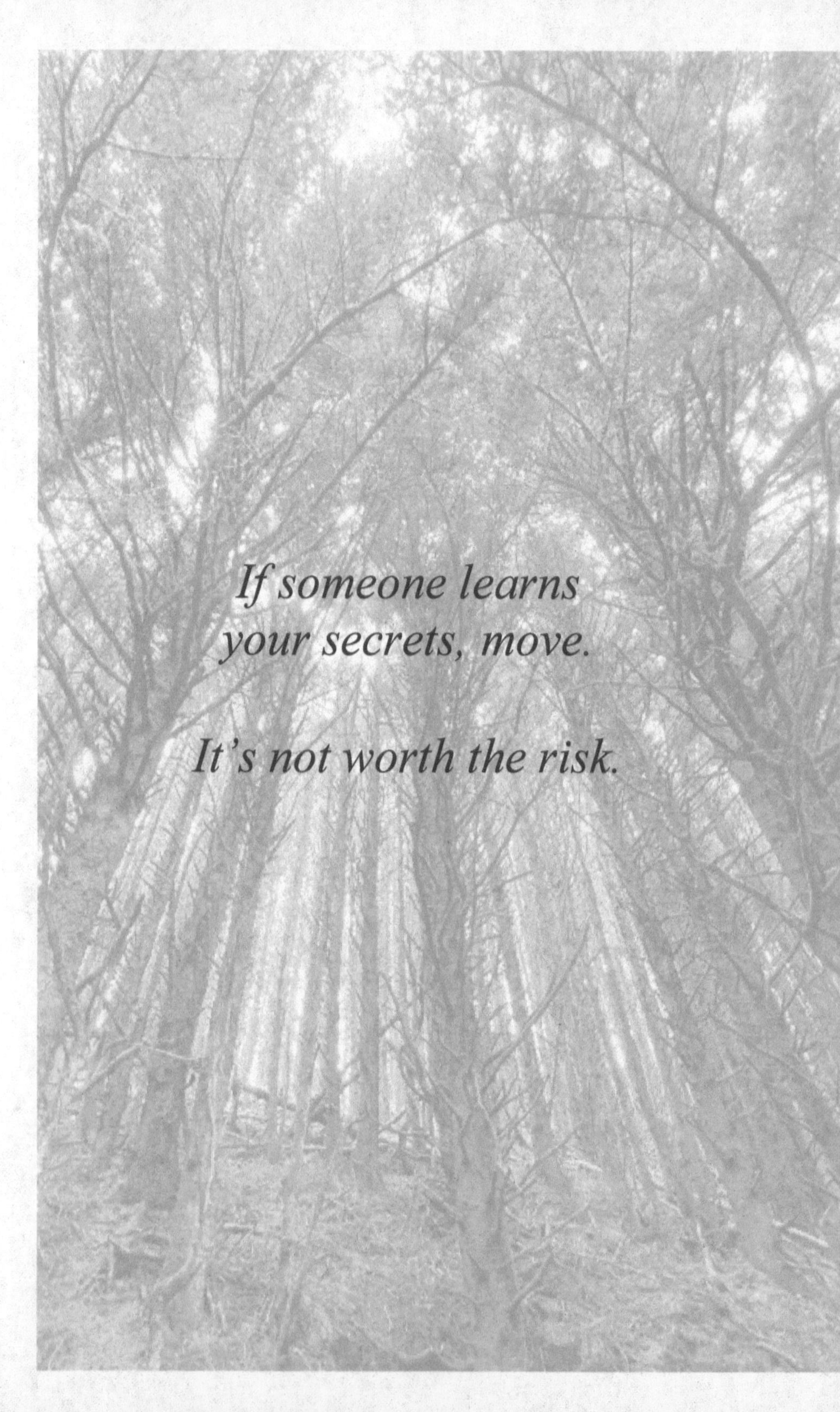
If someone learns
your secrets, move.

It's not worth the risk.

Once you have Transformed,
you are a magnificent creature.

Remember that.

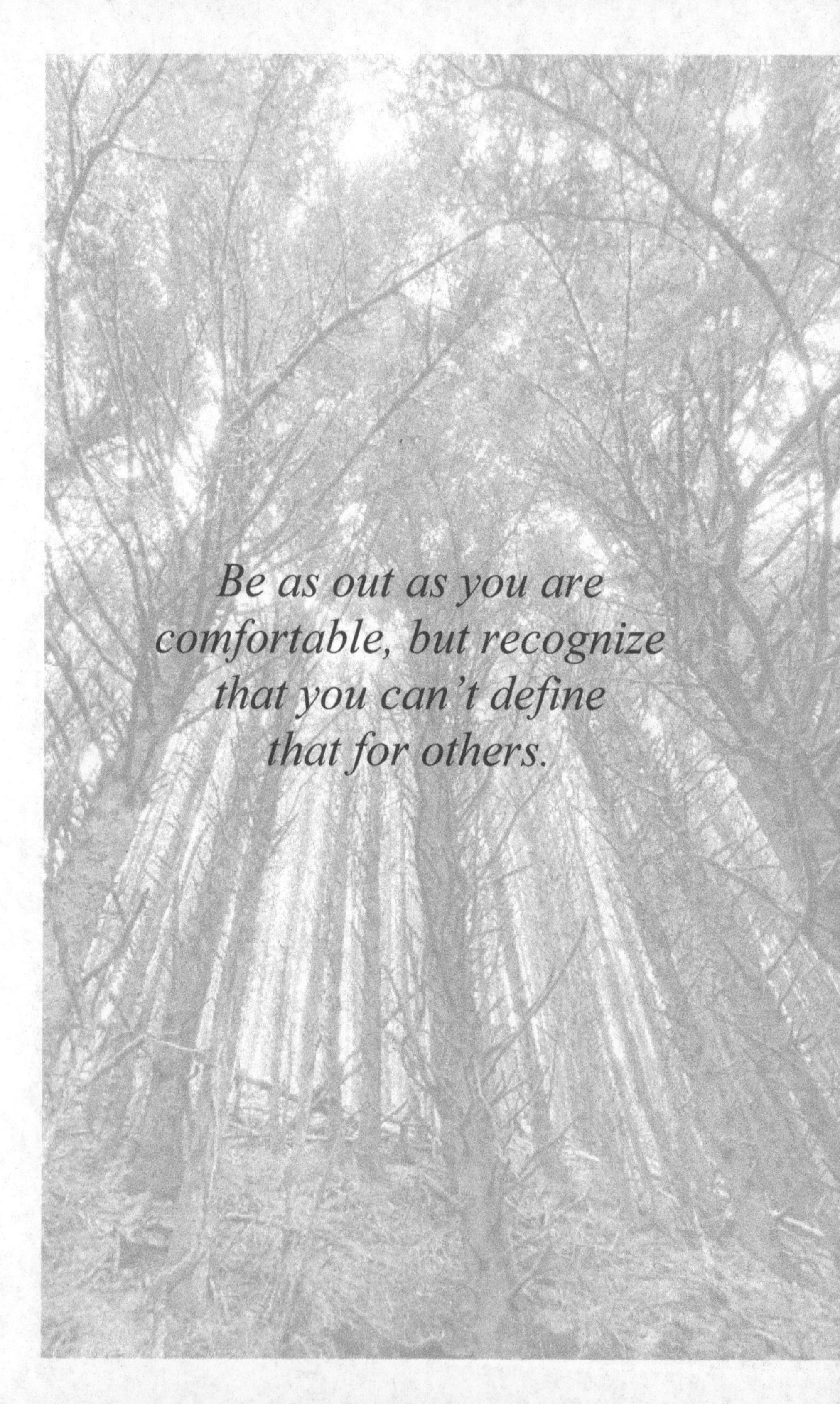

Be as out as you are
comfortable, but recognize
that you can't define
that for others.

A werewolf is an elemental force, and it takes another elemental force to stop you.

Silver is an element.

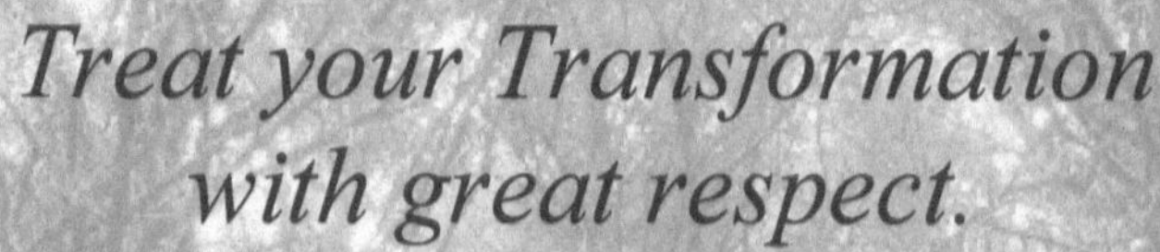

*Treat your Transformation
with great respect.*

*You may feel like playing
basketball, but you can't
unring that bell.*

If someone doesn't make you a
better monster, then maybe
they aren't right for you.

Know your limits:
the chain plus six feet.

Your jaws are strong enough
to break any mold.

Brush and floss every day.

Your teeth are your life.

At the end of your life,
hide your bones.

You deserve the rest.

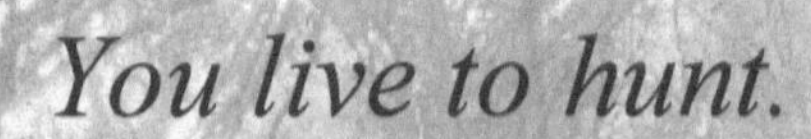

You live to hunt.

*Don't let the world make you
into a book-wolf.*

Buy a house with a basement
so you can make private time
for your needs.

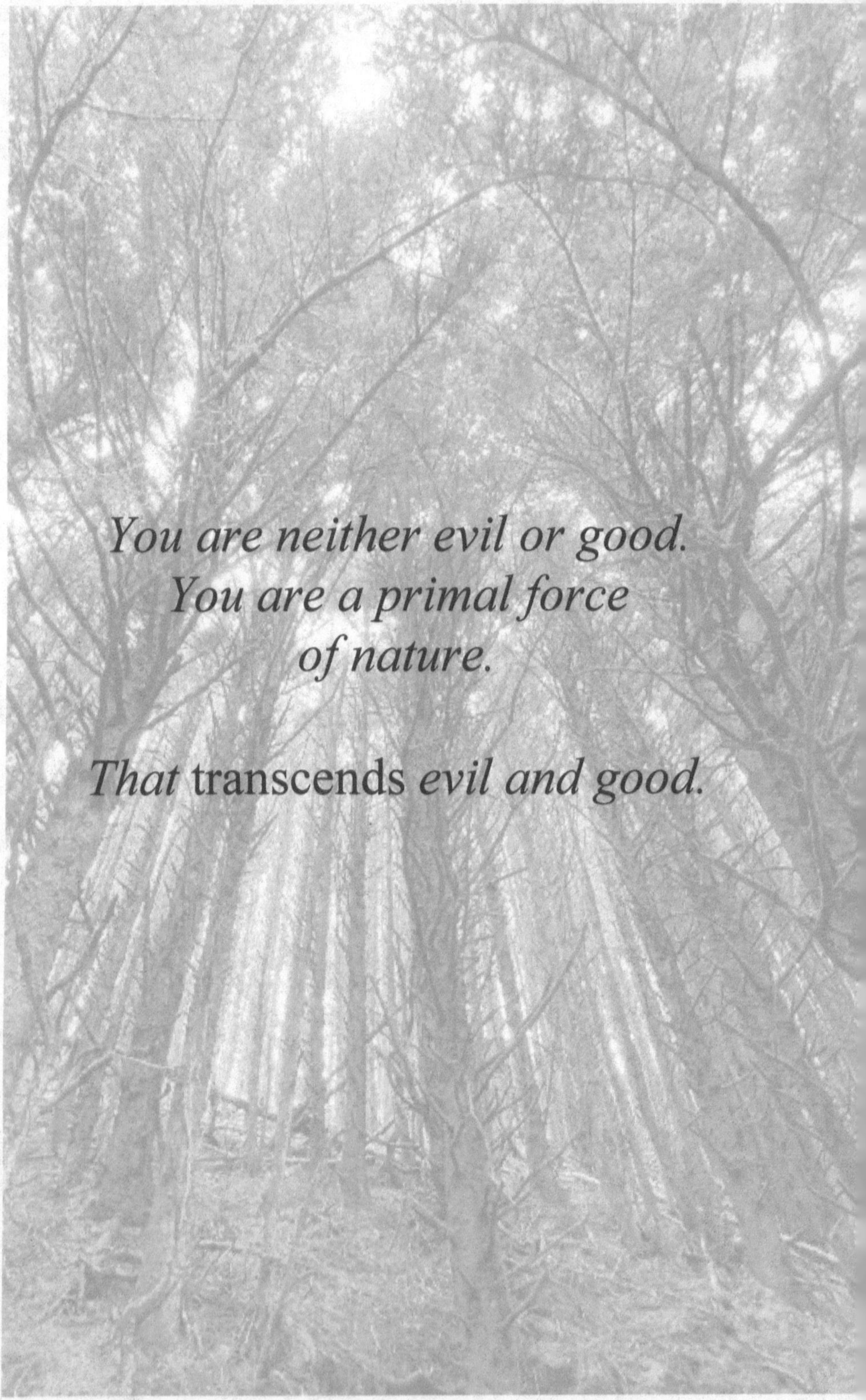

*You are neither evil or good.
You are a primal force
of nature.*

That transcends evil and good.

If you chase a scent, but see no creature, it might be a trap.

Trust all your senses — not just your nose.

It can be cute referring to your Transformation as "having the upholsterers in," but remember that this is your right — no one else can get away with that.

Do not fear being alone.

Sometimes it's best that way.

Everything dies.

It's okay to be the instrument
of that.

If you must bite,
bite to finish the job.

Take no half-bites.

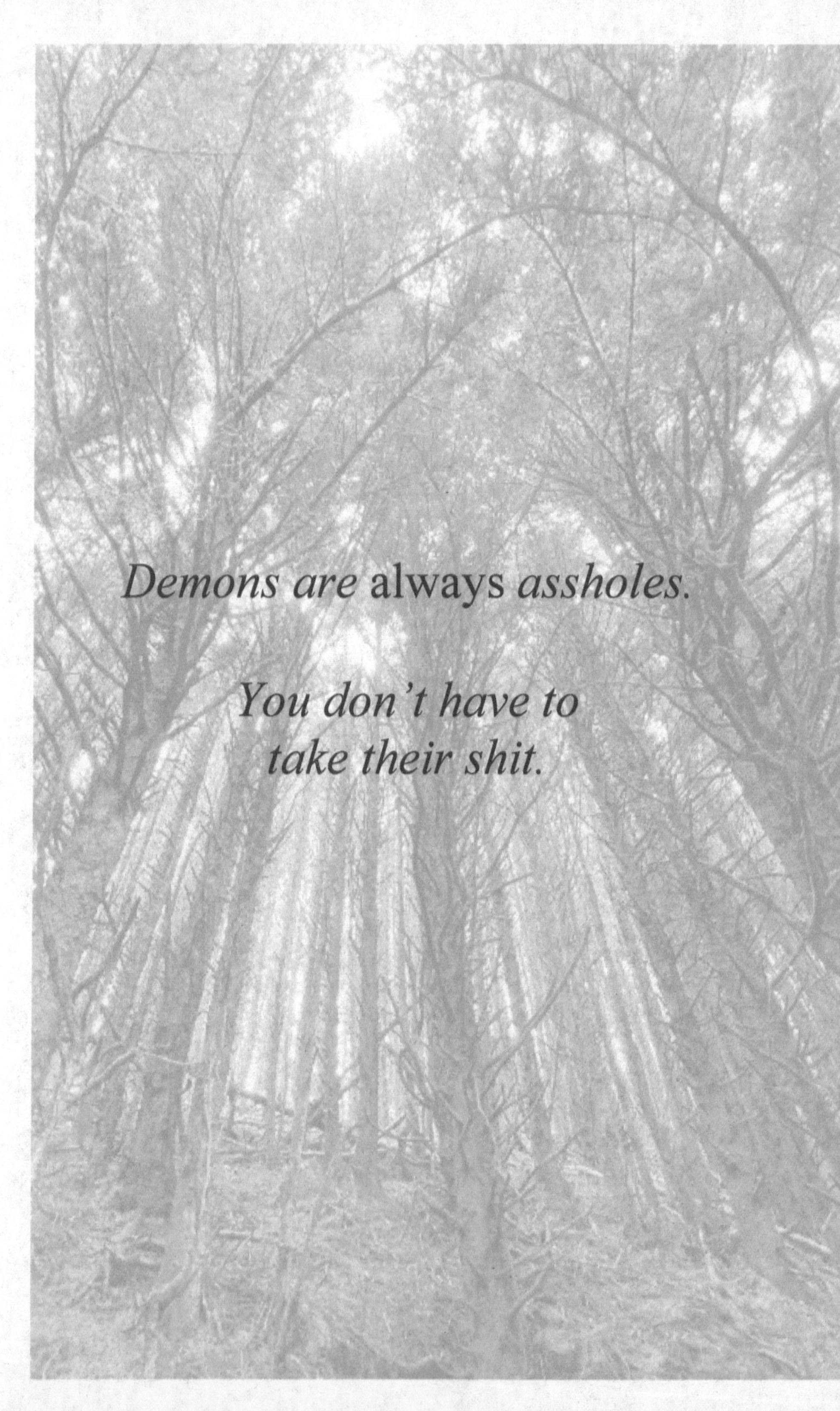
Demons are always assholes.

You don't have to
take their shit.

Wash your paws before you
eat — preferably in the blood
of your kill.

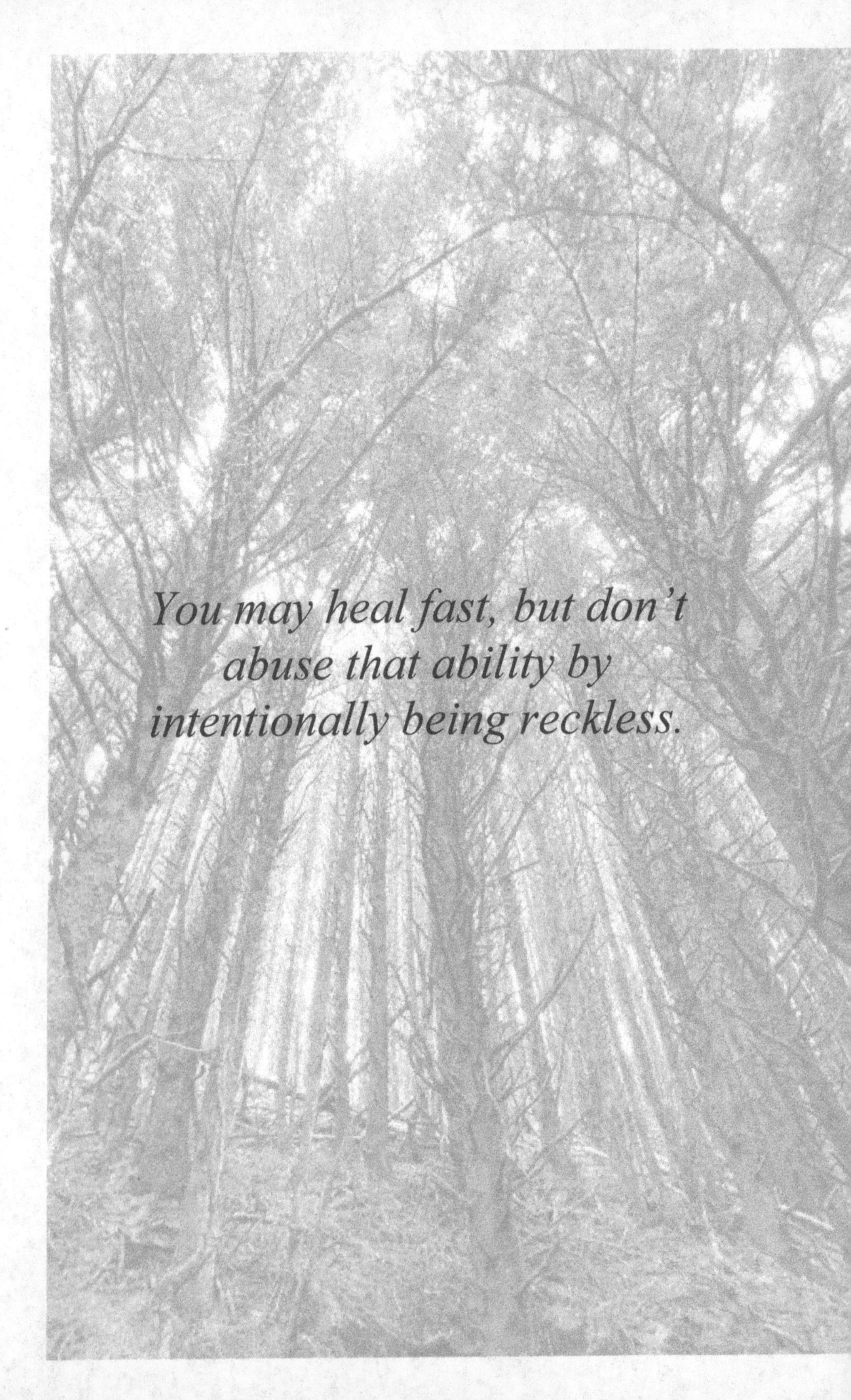
You may heal fast, but don't abuse that ability by intentionally being reckless.

*The Golden Rule is fine,
but pay more attention to
the Silver Rule:*

Avoid all silver.

A lot of humans want to be like
you, but you don't owe them
anything, least of all your gifts.

*Don't judge others by how
many legs they use.*

*Some use four, some use two,
but all are awe-inspiring.*

Stretchy clothes are better.

It doesn't matter if you call yourself a werewolf or a lycanthrope, or whatever — as long as you respect your condition.

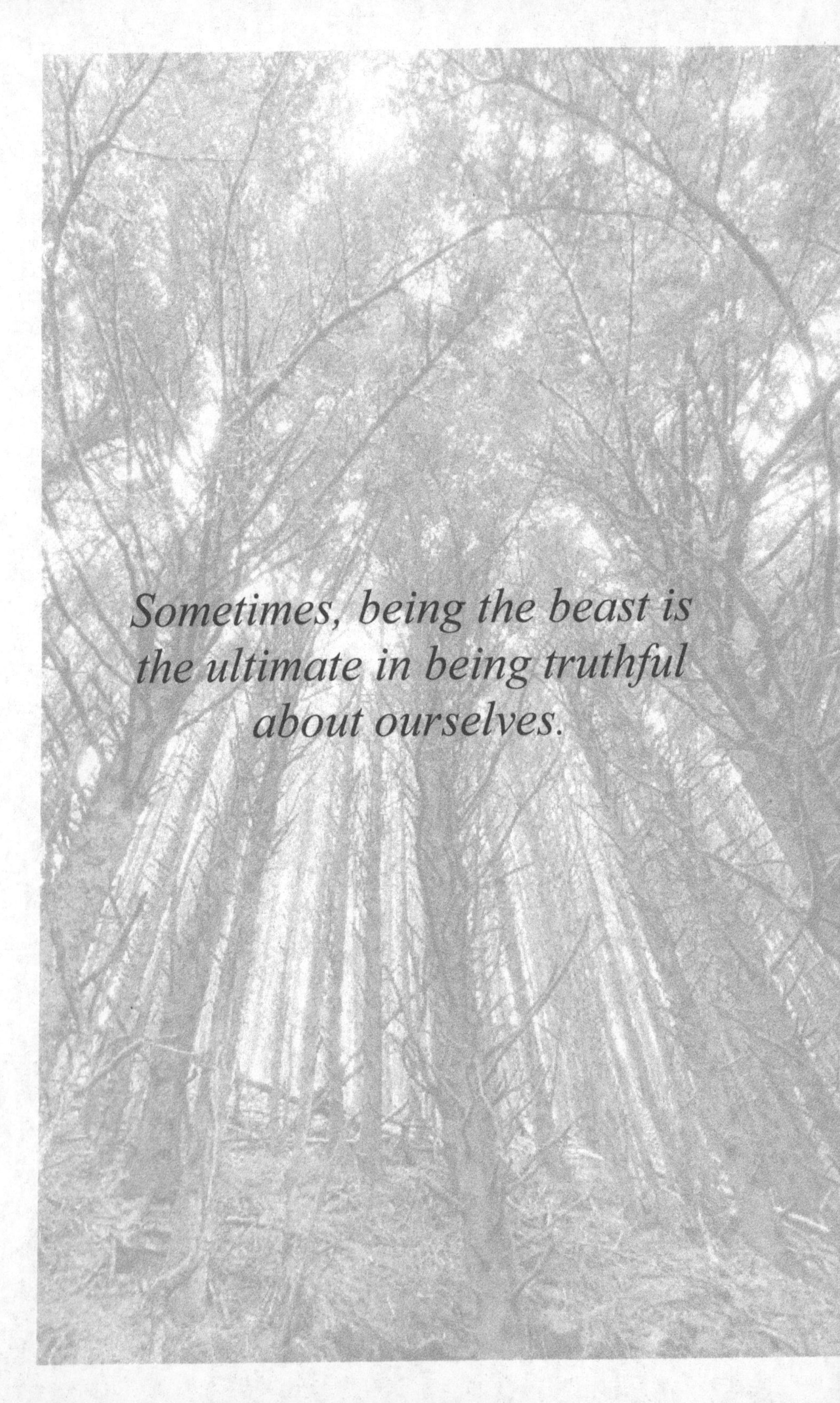
Sometimes, being the beast is
the ultimate in being truthful
about ourselves.

Werewolves aren't new — they are ancient and wondrous.

You are a hunter— always
remember that.

Don't let people goad you into
becoming a beast.

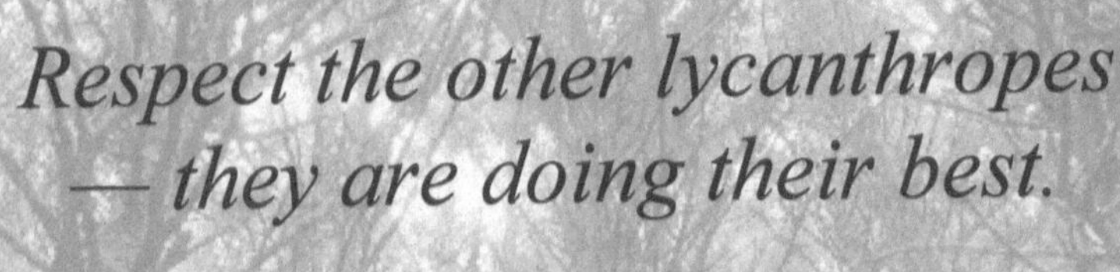

Respect the other lycanthropes — they are doing their best.

We all have our gifts.

Dedicate your entire being
to existing as the
awesome beast you are.

Find balance in your life.

Some folks you let go, and
some folks you kill.

Bodies are like Lego creations:
easier to dispose of once you
separate the pieces.

*Check under the sink for
household chemicals that
contain silver.*

*There are much safer
alternatives.*

*Spectral werewolves are rare
and beautiful.*

*Honor them when you see
them.*

Someday, that may be you.

*You always have family
in the world.*

Always.

*Sometimes you have to wait for
the full moon, but if you listen,
you'll hear them.*

Smell it before you bite it.

Ferocity is purity of purpose.

That is 100% yours.

*Watch your temper — it's too
easy to lose it at bozos.*

Never mate while Transformed.

It's too easy to make mistakes.

You're not a fetish, not a toy,
not an "idea.

You are death incarnate.

*Keep small caches of clothing
outside your house.*

*You might not make it
back by dawn.*

Don't hunt vampires — they can be crafty.

But if a vampire messes with you or yours, shred them.

You smell wonderful.

*If you hear something,
check it out.*

It's never "just the wind."

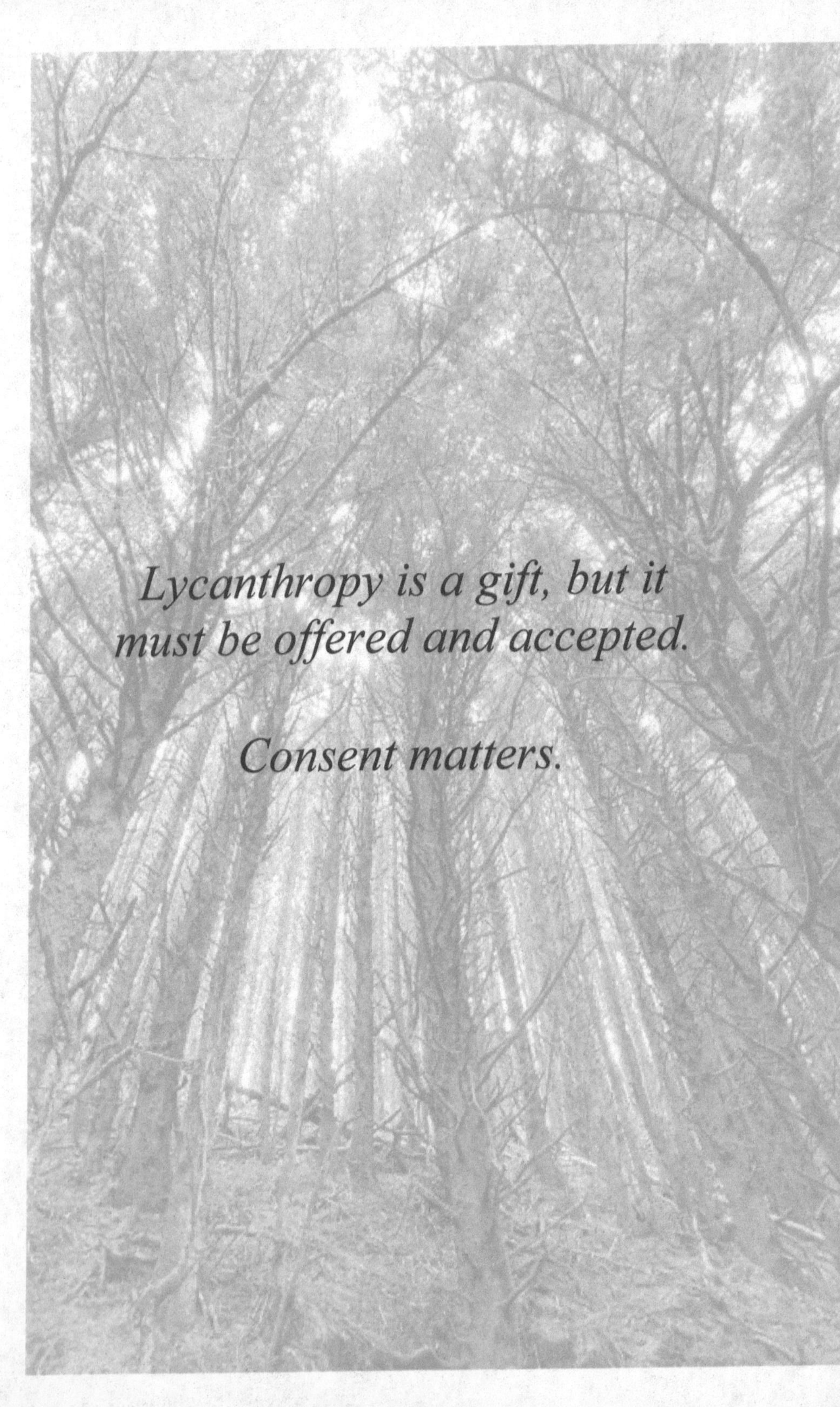
Lycanthropy is a gift, but it must be offered and accepted.

Consent matters.

Iron chains are for the fae.

Break them.

*Chains or fae, whichever
makes sense at the time.*

*Never back away from
being a werewolf.*

*When you reject your true self,
tragic mistakes can happen.*

*Humans don't understand
what it means to push your
boundaries.*

Be the better beast.

Turn the other cheek.

*Unless they deserve it,
of course.*

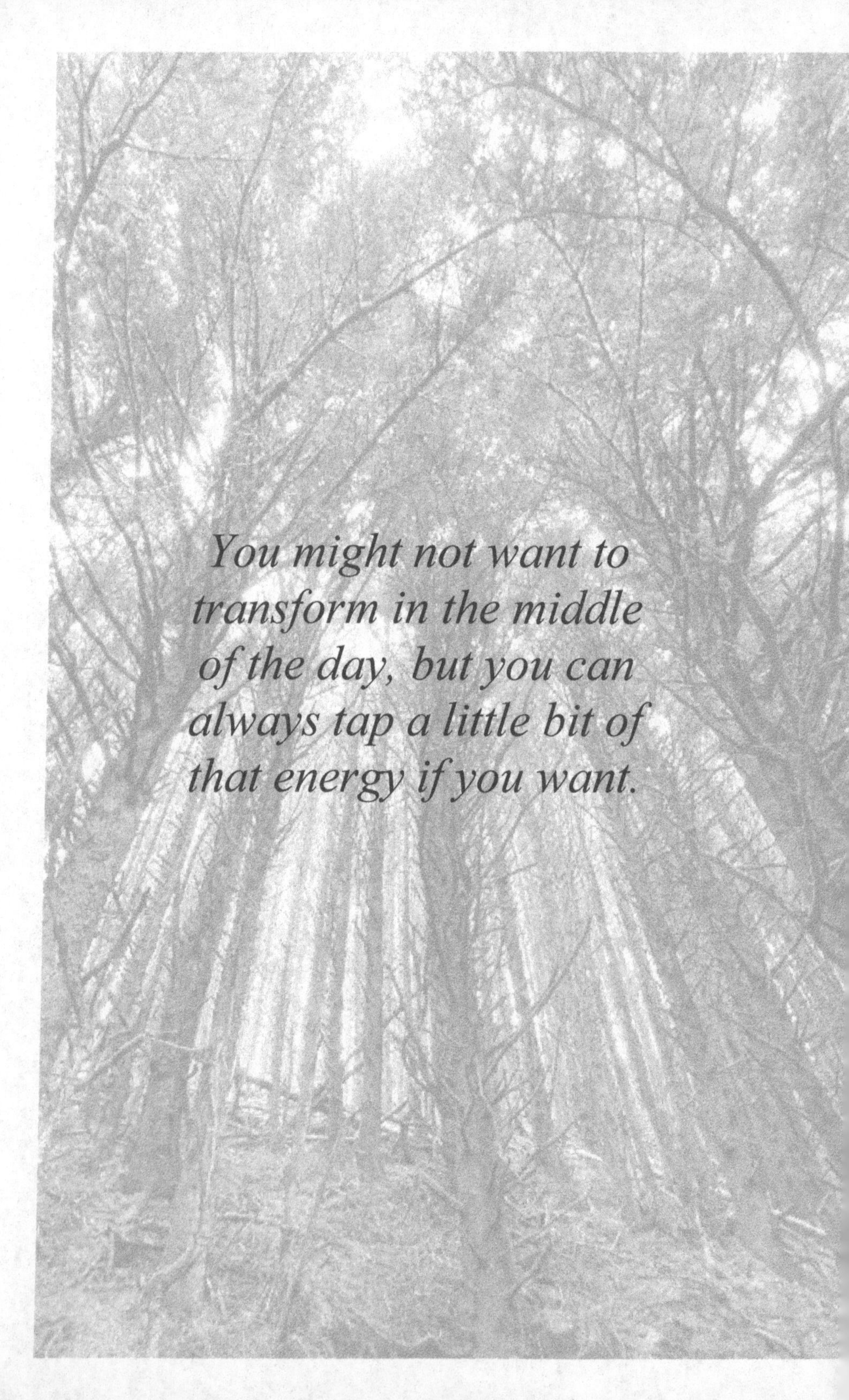

You might not want to
transform in the middle
of the day, but you can
always tap a little bit of
that energy if you want.

Part of what you do is to help pups be better werewolves.

This is a sacred duty.

You're not a dog, you're not a wolf, you're not a human.

You're a beast.

An amazing beast.

Rope can't hold you down.

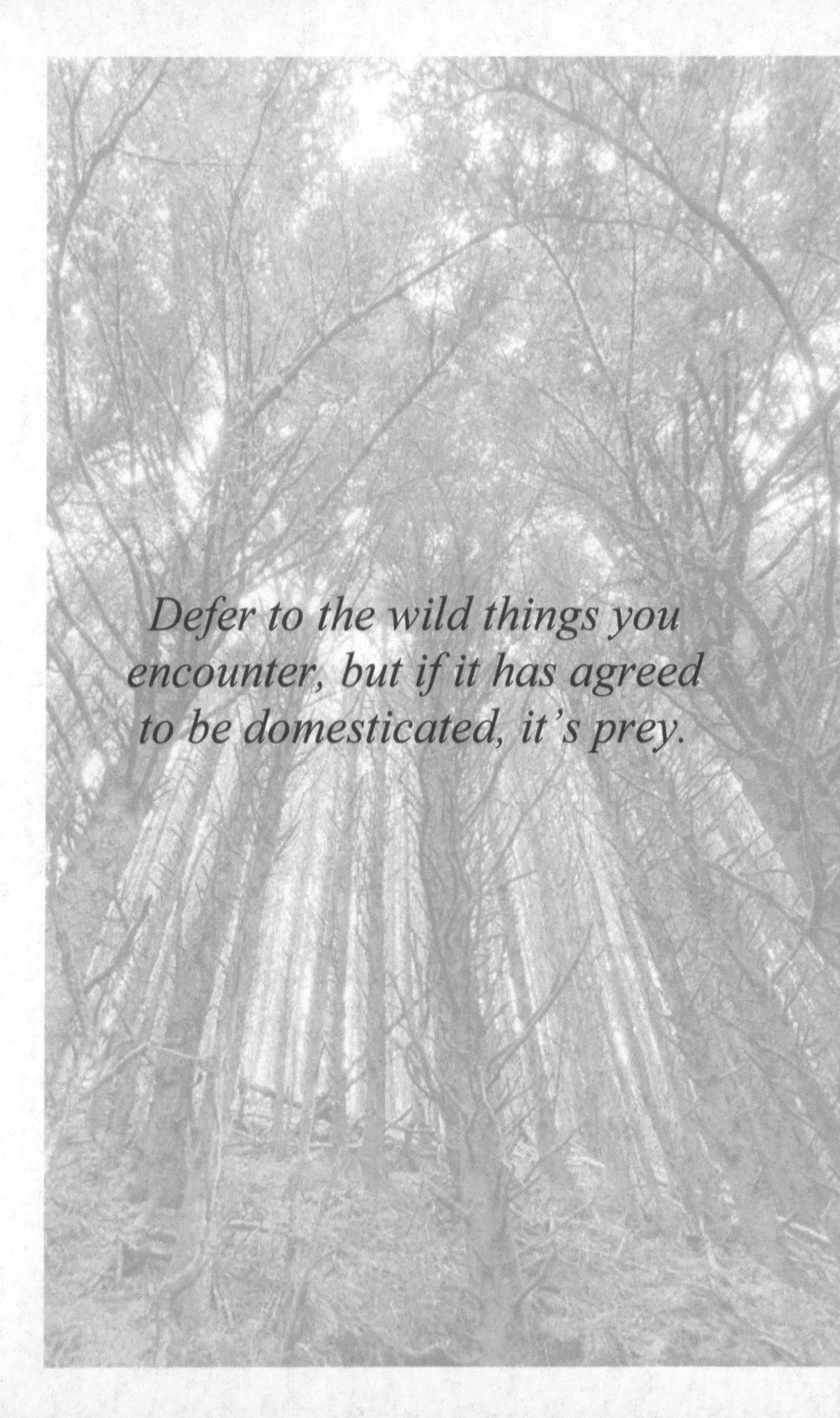
Defer to the wild things you
encounter, but if it has agreed
to be domesticated, it's prey.

If your pack doesn't serve your
needs, leave that pack.

There are other packs.

You don't need to be the Alpha
— the Omega eats, too.

If you must argue, argue, but never let it get out of hand.

Someone will probably die.

Be wary of Rakshasha.

*Their body speaks more truth
than their words.*

*Keep an eye on what
their tail tells you.*

Be confident, but not overconfident.

Some folks just happen to have silver nearby.

You never know.

*If you don't want
to hunt people,
cultivate a field of rabbits.*

Ultimately, it's the same thing.

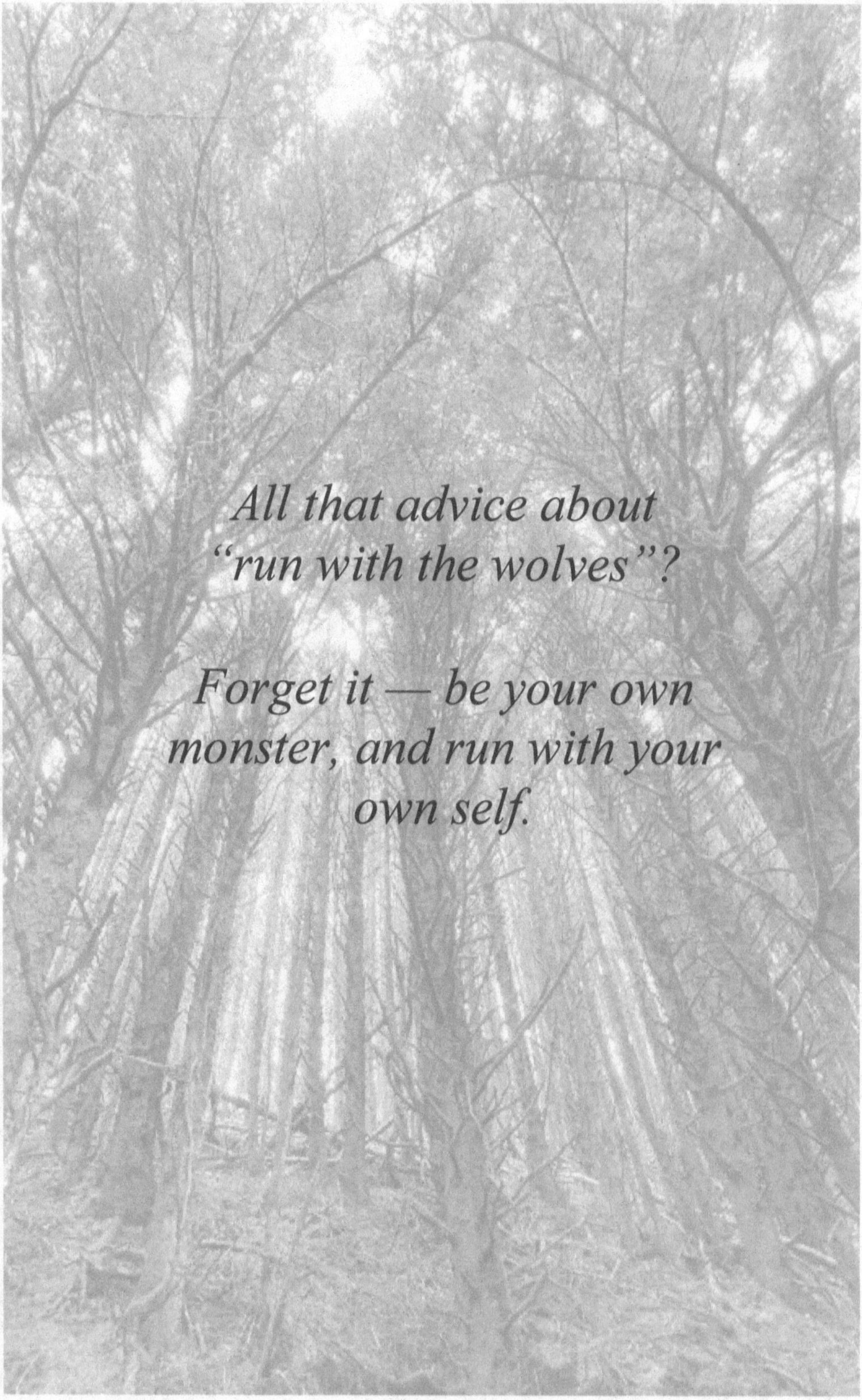

*All that advice about
"run with the wolves"?*

*Forget it — be your own
monster, and run with your
own self.*

Never Transform out of anger.

If you aren't ready to die,
then live.

Life is for taking big bites.

Don't wait to eat tomorrow
what can be eaten today.

Fur can always be
scrubbed clean later.

Enjoy being messy now.

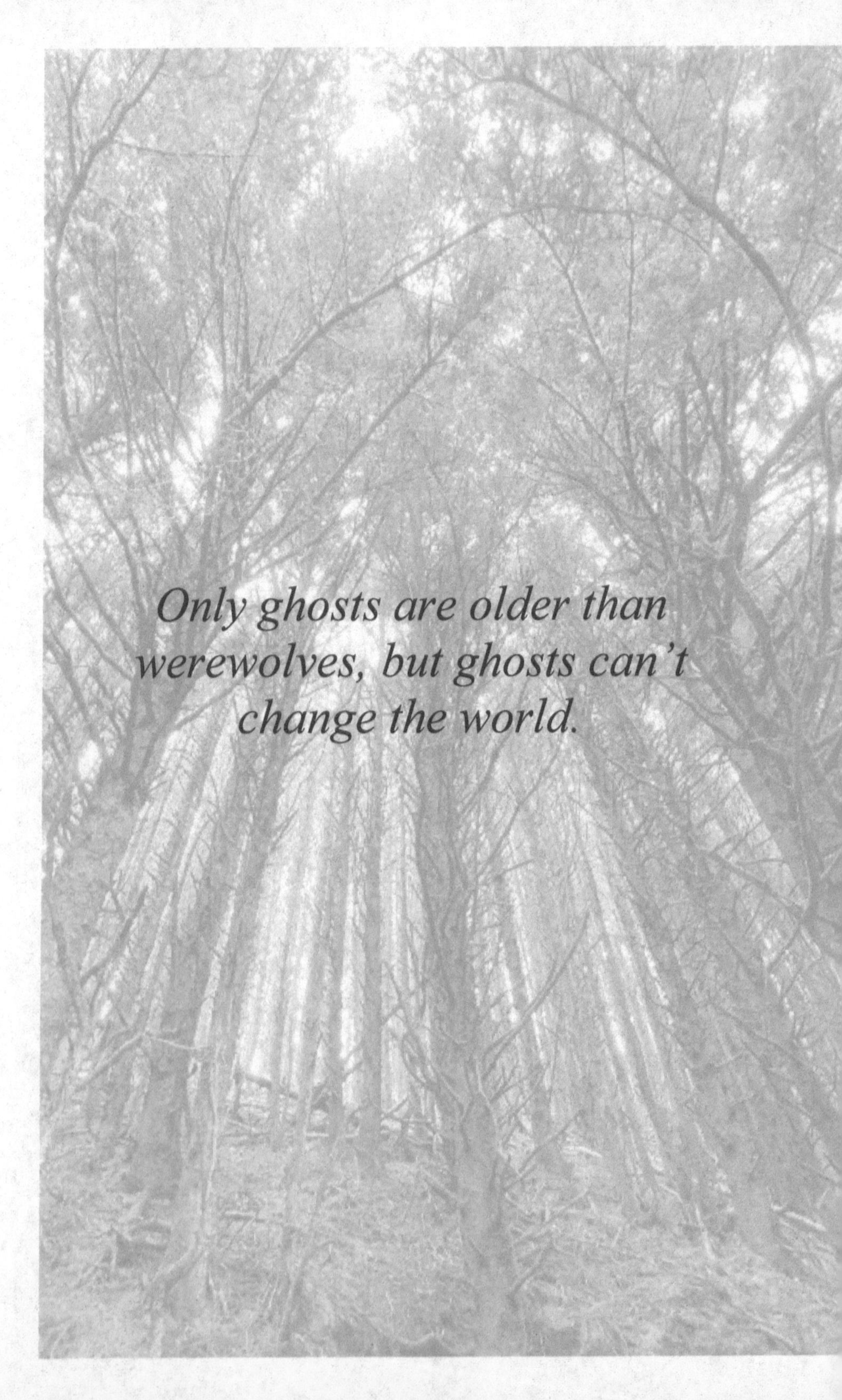

Only ghosts are older than werewolves, but ghosts can't change the world.

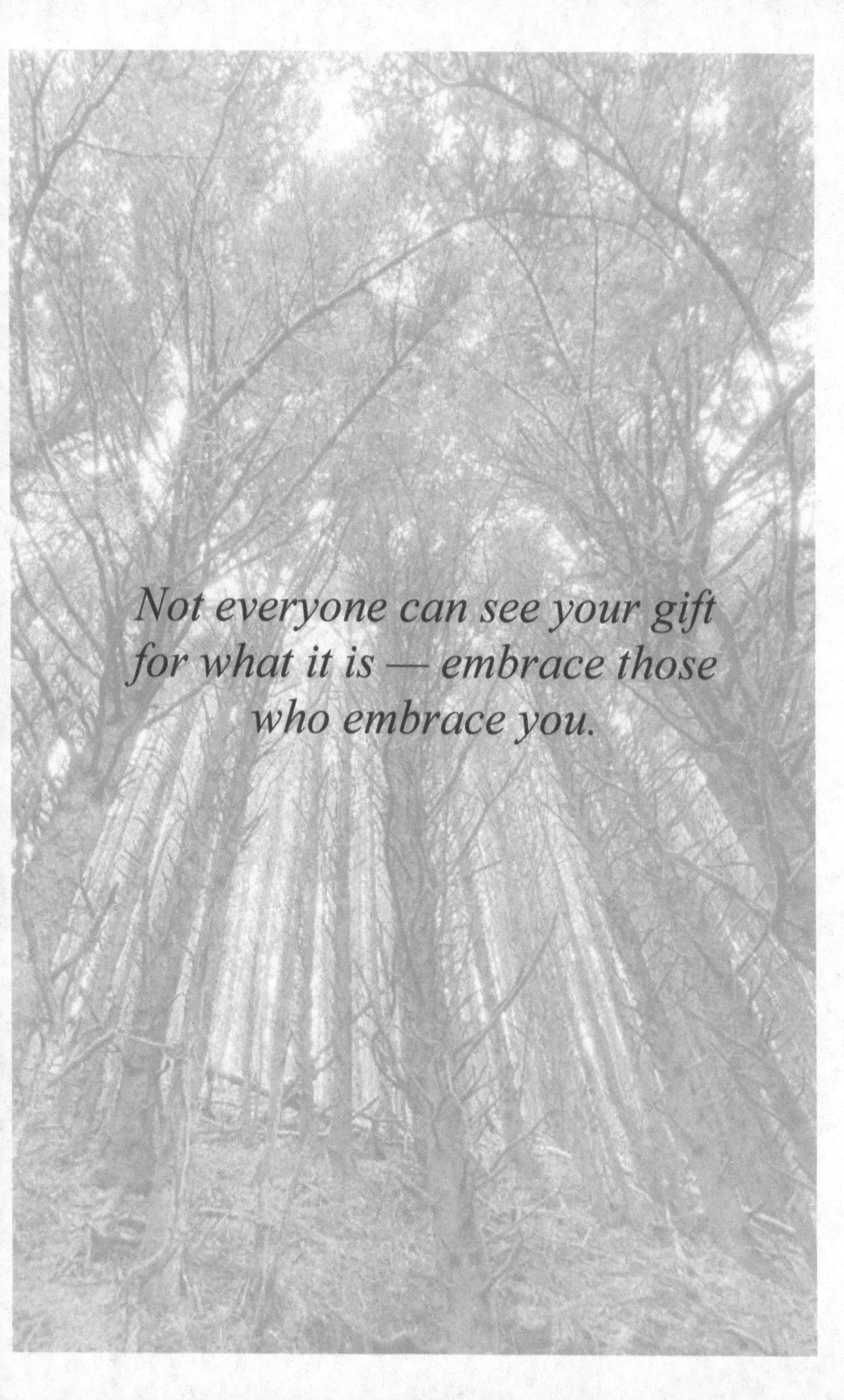
Not everyone can see your gift
for what it is — embrace those
who embrace you.

*When you commit
to an action,
commit ear, tooth and claw.*

*You are not a creature
of half-measures.*

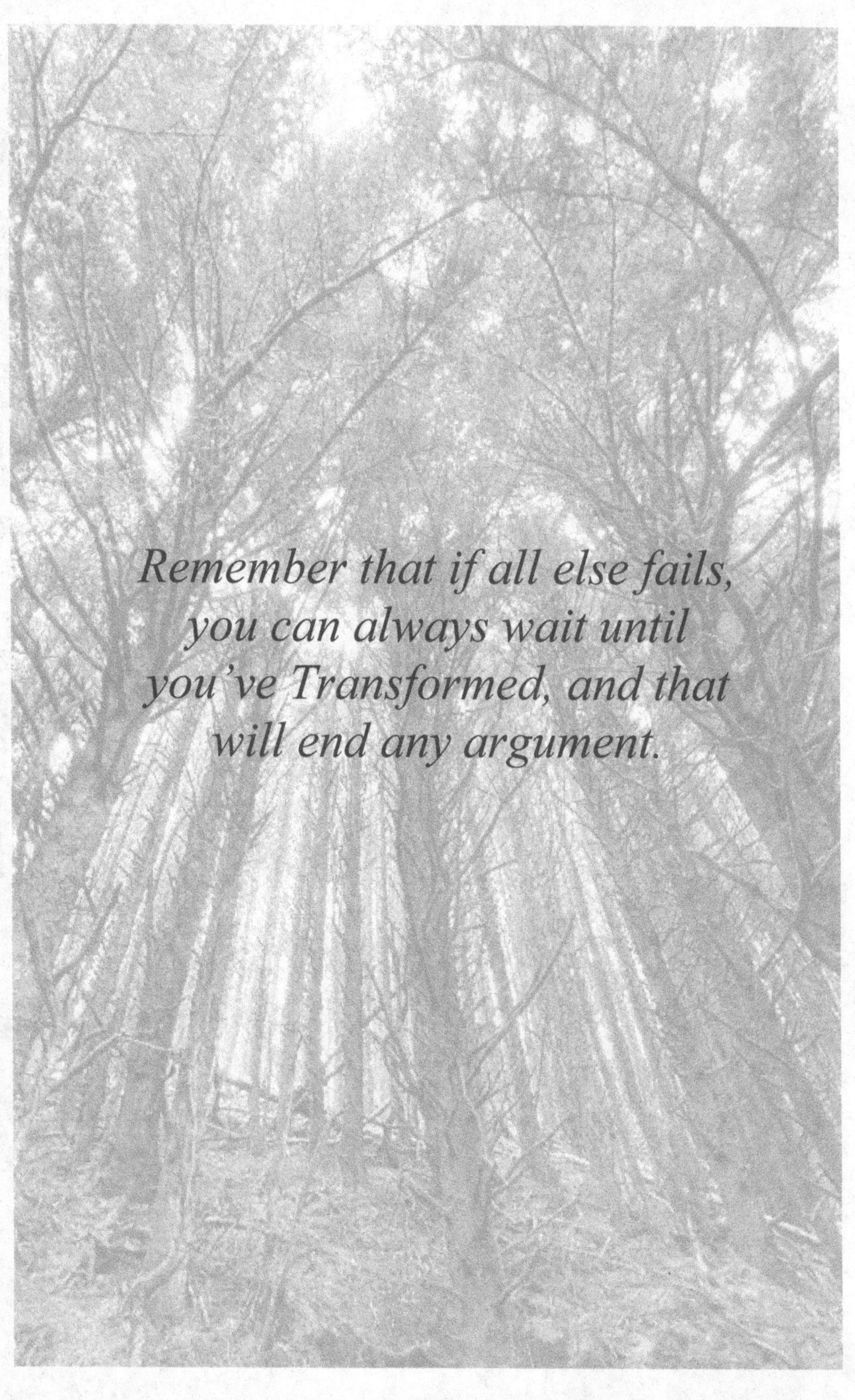

Remember that if all else fails,
you can always wait until
you've Transformed, and that
will end any argument.

Respect puppies.

Even when they are trying.

Very trying

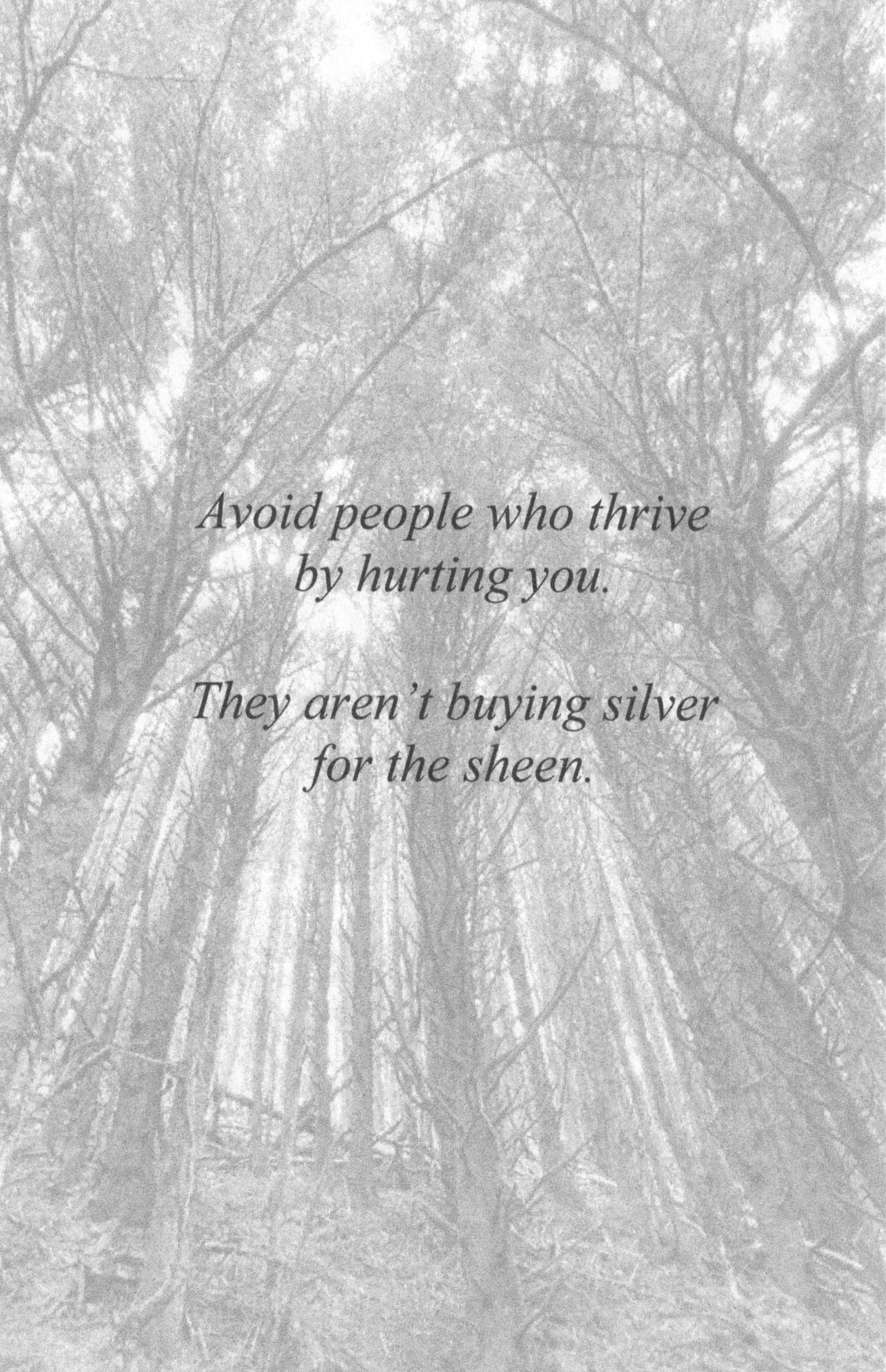
Avoid people who thrive
by hurting you.

They aren't buying silver
for the sheen.

*Humans have no idea
what it's like being you.*

*It's okay to let them live with
their illusions.*

Don't mock your
Transformation.

Respect it.

Fear has a smell.

Learn it!

If your partner can't handle
you at your worst,
then eat them.

*There is no beast in the history
of history itself that is more
natural than a werewolf.*

Be proud.

Don't keep silver things at your house.

Why tempt fate?

*For some folks, killin' them isn't
worth dulling your claws.*

Be picky.

You have two birthdays — one
when you were born, and one
when you were reborn.

Don't leave loose ends.

Follow up every bite.

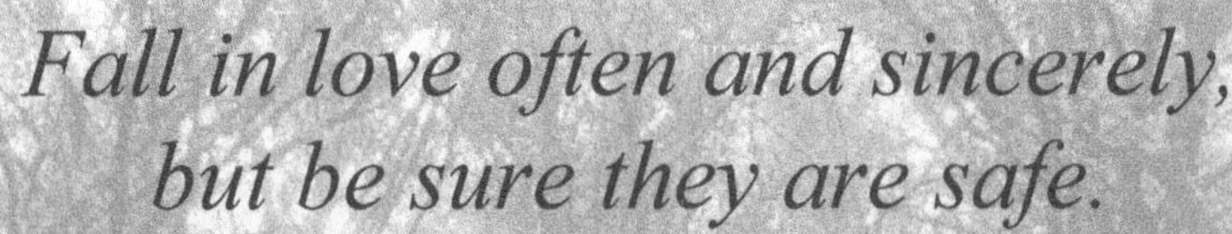

*Fall in love often and sincerely,
but be sure they are safe.*

The attic is safe.

Mostly.

Werewolves don't owe their existence to radioactive goop, aliens, or any of that foolishness.

They are 100% natural.

Don't bite unless you have to.

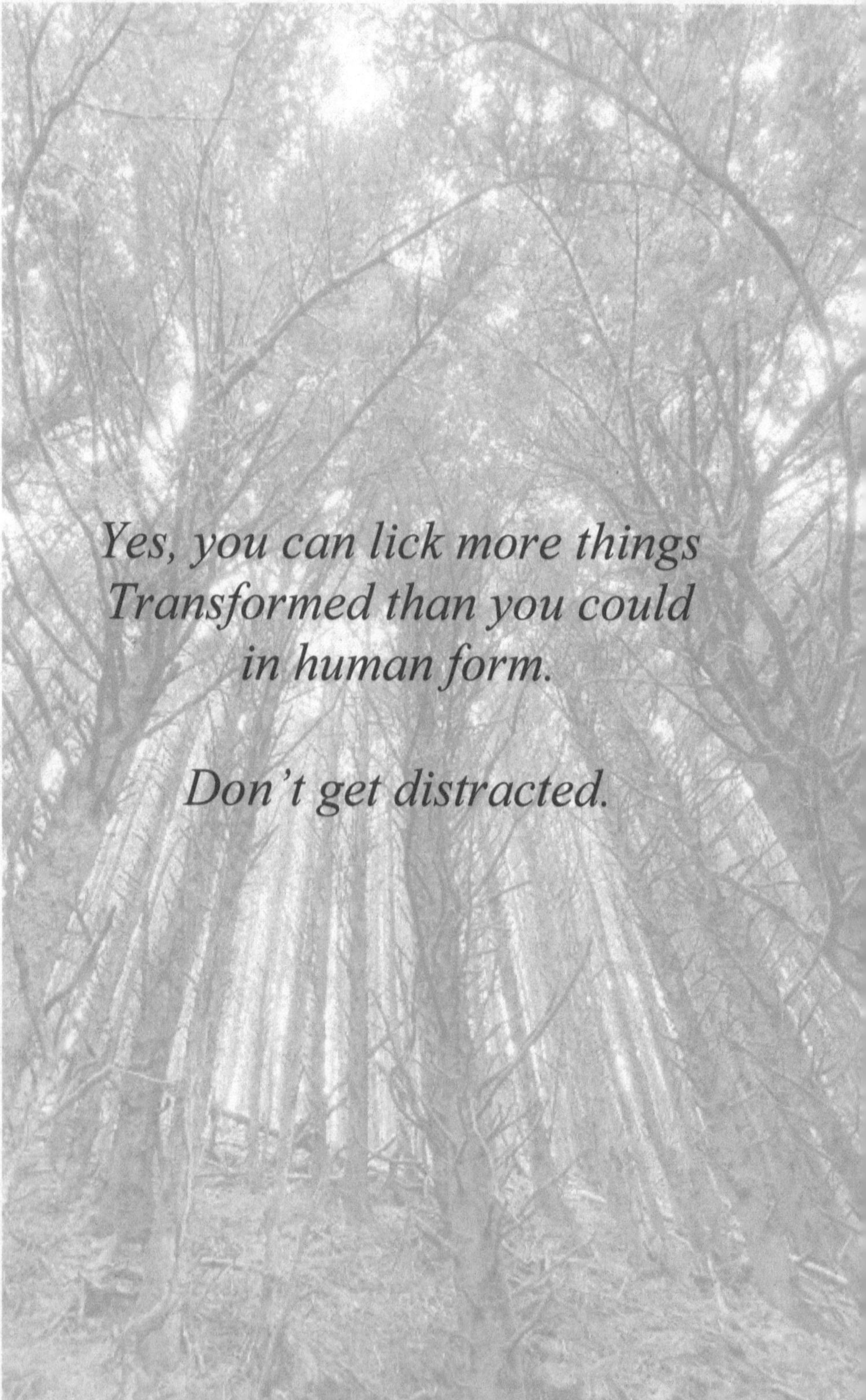

*Yes, you can lick more things
Transformed than you could
in human form.*

Don't get distracted.

You will always have enemies.

Be canny, be wary,
but don't let fear rule you.

Werewolves are Nature's
justice machines.

*If you join a pack,
respect them.*

*They were there
before you were.*

There is no "old-school" versus "new school" werewolf competition.

All werewolves are "ancient school" and glorious.

Don't be sexist.

Eat a balanced diet.

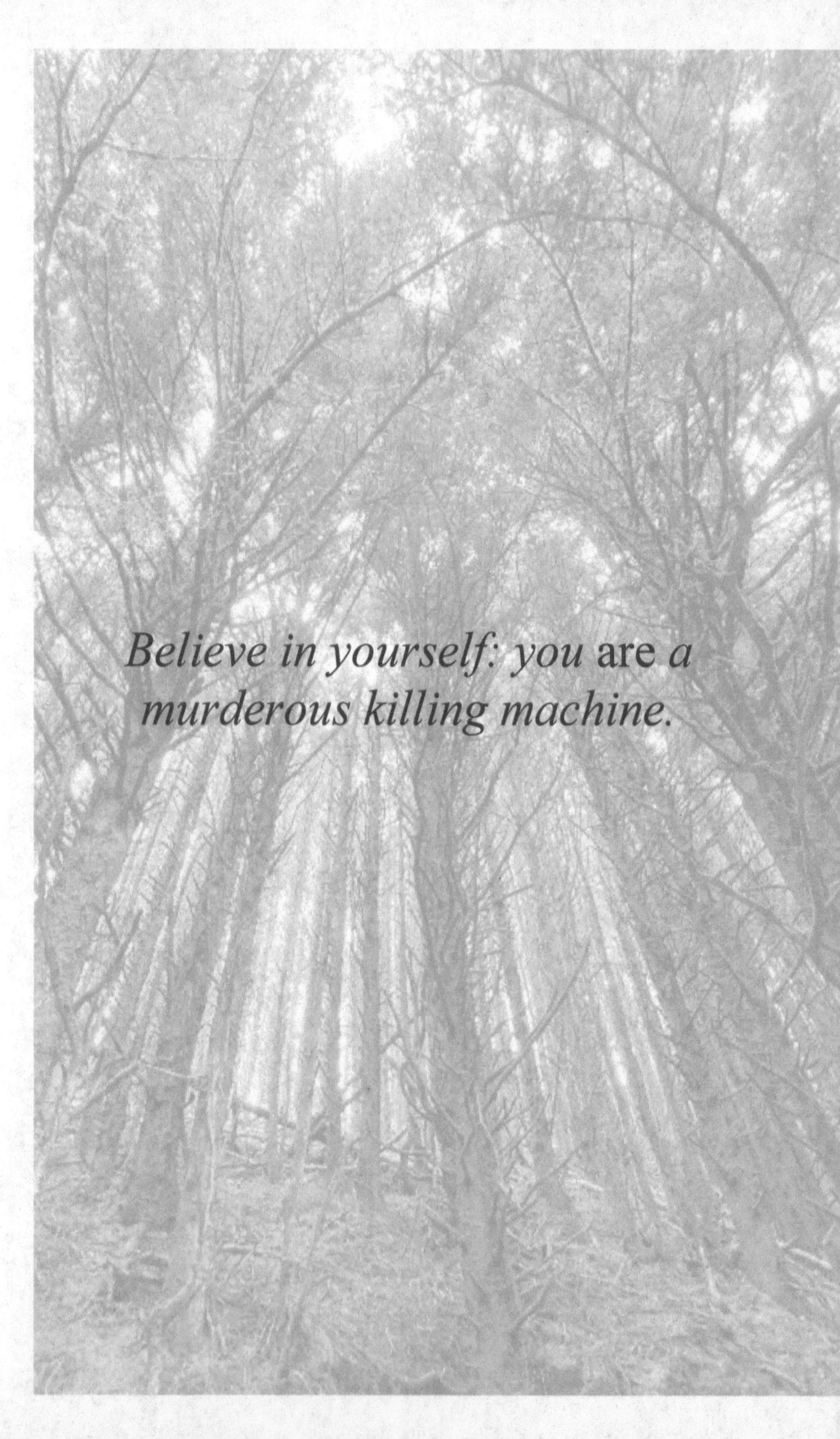
Believe in yourself: you are a
murderous killing machine.

*You are of an ancient race, but
you aren't some hick.*

*Be a modern mechanism
of death.*

*Hunting is an activity,
not a lifestyle.*

*Don't get so caught up in it
that you forget where you are.*

Ignore cawing crows.

They are all feather, no bone.

Don't get caught red-fanged.

Bury your kills.

Your Transformation is an
extraordinary time for you.

Embrace it!

Don't be racist.

*Everybody is delicious once
you learn to appreciate
their flavors.*

*Once a month, you are the
most genuine predator
in existence.*

*But the secret is: during the
rest of your time, you are, too.*

Pick your targets.
Never kill indiscriminately.

Don't be jealous of vampires.

They may be immortal,
but they are super glum.

If you want to be serious,
use chains.

*Nobody cares that the "silver"
isn't real silver — as long as
you're a good cook.*

Cultivate camouflage skills.

Don't turn into a monster
when someone you love
is in the room.

Don't be simply a werewolf—
be a self-awarewolf.

*People will call you savage and
ruthless as if it is an insult.*

*But their jealousy is
not your problem.*

The law of tooth and claw
means that you make the law.

*If you are two-legged after you
Transform, remember that a
heavy overcoat makes you
look just like a human.*

Transformation is a painful
process, but you come out
better in the end.

Never lie about who you are,
unless they can kill you.

Set a time limit on hunting.

If you can't catch it after
the time limit,
you probably never will.

*It doesn't matter if you are
male, female,
or something else.*

*Sex and gender may be fluid,
but once we Transform,
we are all kin.*

Eat what you kill.

Don't leave your mess for
others to clean up.

*Take advantage of
circumstances.*

*Invite troublesome people over
when you know you'll be
Transforming.*

If it smells too good to be true,
it probably is.

Once you're a monster,
even love is ignored.

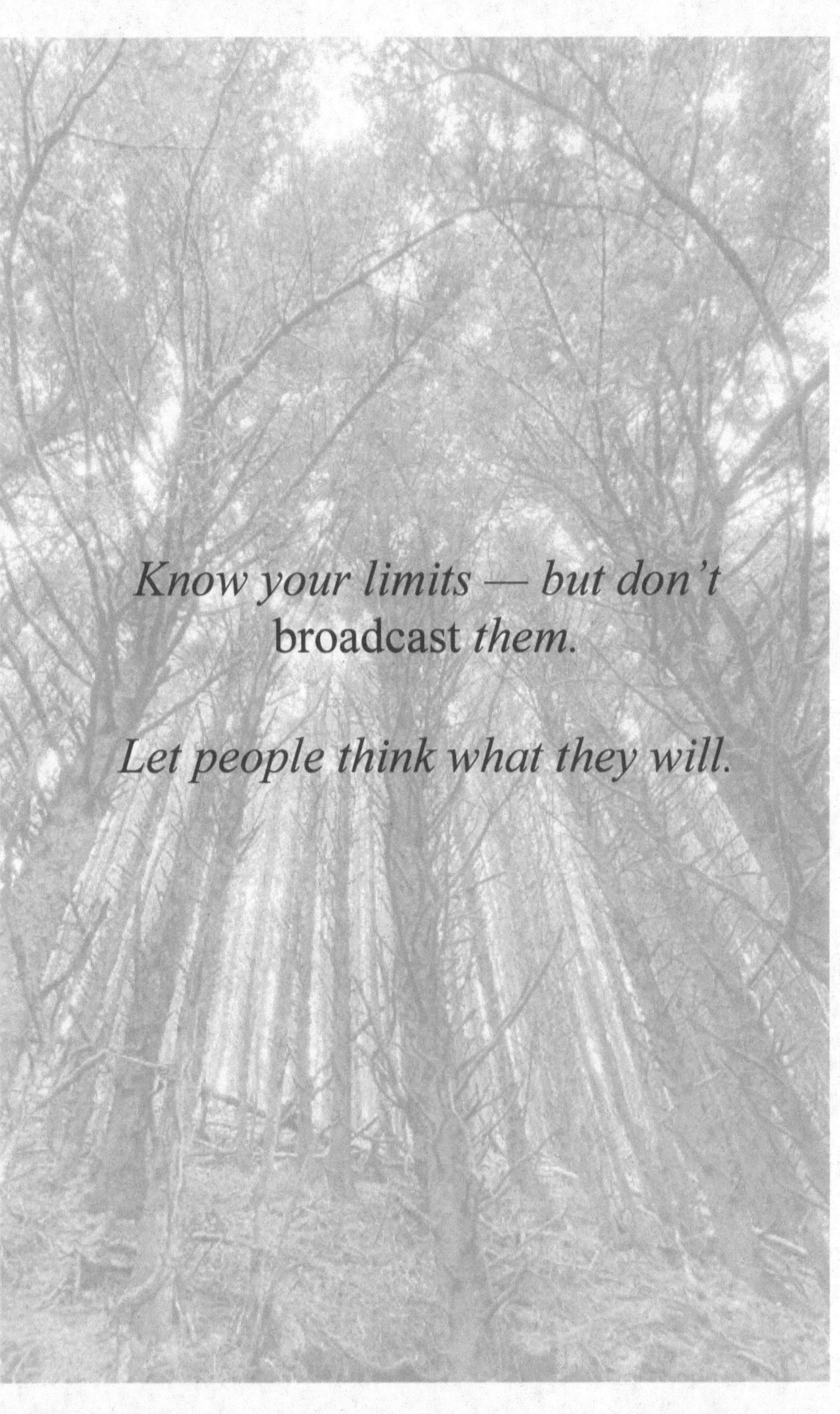
Know your limits — but don't broadcast *them.*

Let people think what they will.

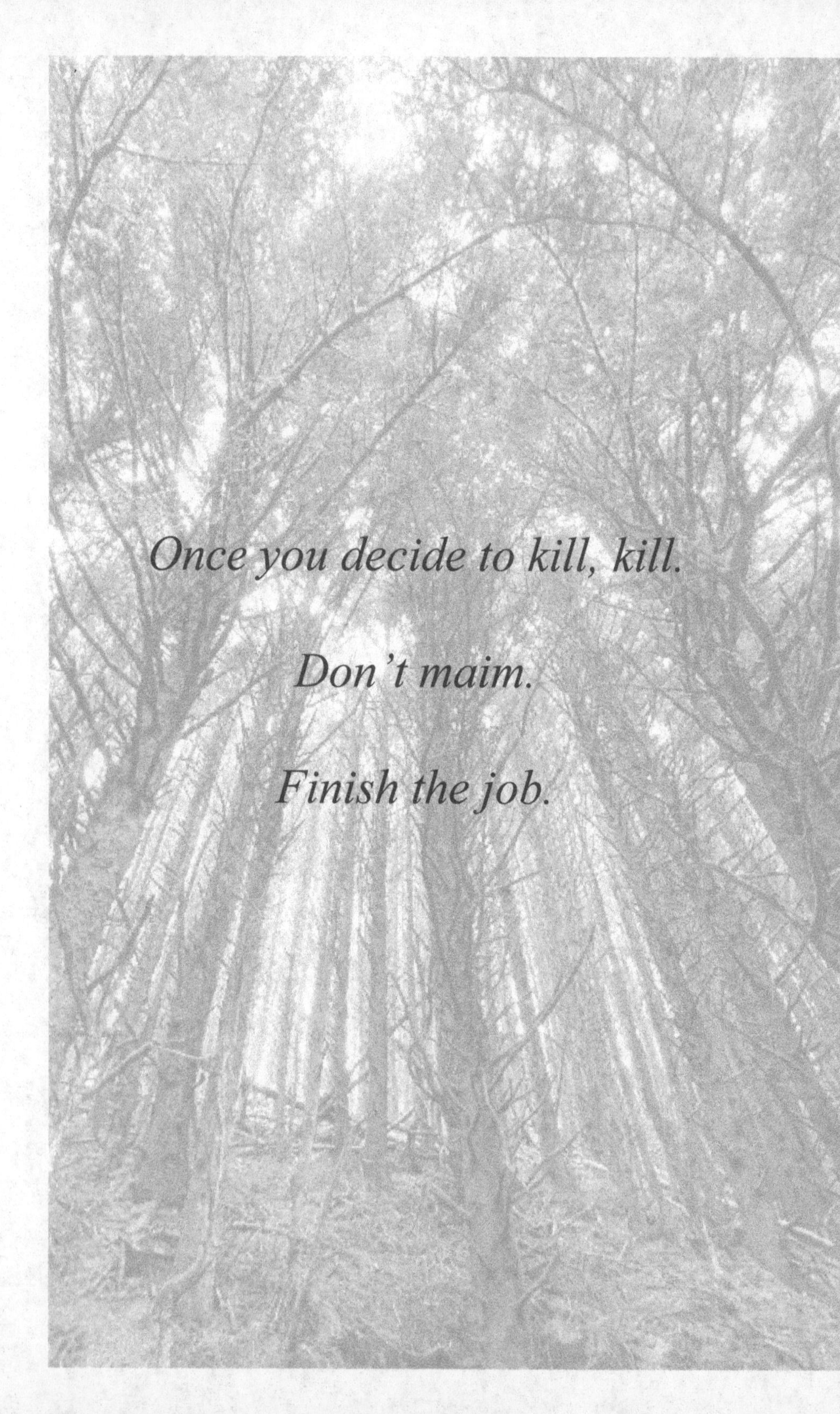
Once you decide to kill, kill.

Don't maim.

Finish the job.

Don't hit people — you have
teeth and claws for a reason.

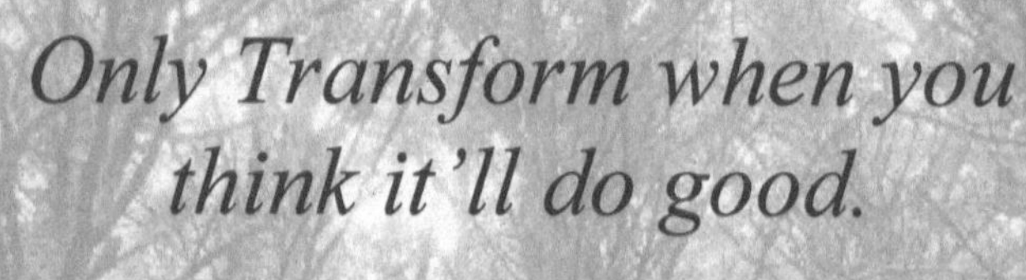

Only Transform when you think it'll do good.

Good for you counts.

Decisions made by tooth and
claw are sincere.

About the Author

Edward Martin III is a writer, a filmmaker, and a calculated risk. He lairs among the sullen boughs and heavy clouds of the Pacific Northwest.

His work includes the novel *Through the Night*, the collection *Close Your Eyes*, the animated Lovecraft feature film *The Dream-Quest of Unknown Kadath*, the groundbreaking zombie movie *Flesh of my Flesh*, the unique drama film *The Dead*, and literally hundreds of episodes of various web series.

Check out HellbenderMedia.com for more info!

Other Works

This other work may delight you.

Through the Night

A breakneck-paced novel about a dark and desperate race for survival, told from the point of view of people in the way.

Close Your Eyes

Fifty-five intriguing and evocative tales of dark mischief, mystery, and mayhem.

The Dream-Quest of Unknown Kadath

An animated adaptation of H. P. Lovecraft's turn-of-the-century fantasy novel.

Hacked Off

A hilarious card game where each player – as a disgraced zombie – tries to rebuild their body and take over leadership of the zombie tribe

Shop at HellbenderMedia.com

The Publisher

Hellbender Media (HellbenderMedia.com) offers rare and voracious entertainment for the reader who prefers the Unusual, including books, movies, games, and other fun things, as well as offering workshops, tutorials, and lots of interactivity with their fans.

Please visit HellbenderMedia.com to learn more!

The Final Word

I had no idea how much this was needed until I started writing.

Ever get that way? That feeling to write that is so strong you work through the night, all the way through to the next day, when you hear the birds and realize you pulled an all-nighter, but you don't even remotely care?

That's a great feeling.

And I keep thinking up more of these, too. Or am I hearing them? I think once you start paying attention, you hear a lot more than you ever thought possible.

Go out tonight, would you? Find a place that is a bit wild and sit in the dark and listen. I expect you may hear some things as well.

Pray they don't hear *you*, of course.